W9-AZJ-960

My The Dog Dinosaur

by Jackie French

illustrated by Stephen Michael King

Librarian Reviewer
Marci Peschke
Librarian, Dallas Independent School District
MA Education Reading Specialist, Stephen F. Austin State University
Learning Resources Endorsement, Texas Women's University

Reading Consultant
Sherry Klehr
Elementary/Middle School Educator, Edina Public Schools, MN
MA in Education, University of Minnesota

STONE ARCH BOOKS
Minneapolis   San Diego

First published in the United States in 2007
by Stone Arch Books,
151 Good Counsel Drive, P.O. Box 669,
Mankato, Minnesota 56002
www.stonearchbooks.com

First published in English in Sydney, Australia,
by HarperCollins Publishers Australia Pty Ltd in 2003.
This English language edition is published by arrangement
with HarperCollins Publishers Australia Pty Ltd.

Library of Congress Cataloging-in-Publication Data
French, Jackie.
    My Dog the Dinosaur / by Jackie French; illustrated by Stephen
Michael King.
        p. cm. — (Funny Families)
        "Pathway Books."
        Summary: Gunk and his family get an unusual-looking puppy from
the animal shelter, but when it grows up to be a dinosaur, no one can
believe it.
        ISBN-13: 978-1-59889-344-1 (library binding)
        ISBN-10: 1-59889-344-0 (library binding)
        ISBN-13: 978-1-59889-437-0 (paperback)
        ISBN-10: 1-59889-437-4 (paperback)
        [1. Dinosaurs—Fiction. 2. Family life—Fiction.] I. King, Stephen
Michael, ill. II. Title.
PZ7.F88903Mz 2007
[Fic]—dc22   2006027145

1 2 3 4 5 6 12 11 10 09 08 07

Printed in the United States of America

Table of Contents

Table of Contents
Continued

CHAPTER 1
A Little, Lonely Dog

He was the loneliest, saddest dog Gunk had ever seen. He sat in the corner of the animal shelter and stared at Gunk.

"I want that one," said Gunk, pointing to the puppy in the corner.

It wasn't much of a dog. It had pale brown fur with dark brown spots, a long neck, and a funny, fat tail.

It didn't even have any ears that Gunk could see. It was sitting all alone in the corner of the big cage, like none of the other dogs wanted anything to do with it.

"Here, boy!" Gunk called to the dog.

The dog wagged its big, fat tail. "Spt," said the dog.

"It can't even bark," said Mom, sighing.

"Come here, dog," said Gunk. The dog trotted toward him. Gunk knew that he and the dog were made for each other.

"Spt," said the dog.

Dad sighed. "Okay," he said. "Let's go pay for it."

CHAPTER 2

Spot Comes Home

The dog was quiet on the way home. It snuggled into Gunk's lap in the back of the car.

The car pulled up in the driveway. Gunk opened the door. "See? We're home," Gunk said to the dog.

"Spt," said the dog, drooling as it peered out the window.

"This is our yard for you to play in," said Gunk. "And that's the neighbor's cat for you to chase."

"Sptttttttttt!" yelped the dog. It snuggled back into Gunk's arms and hid its face in his shirt.

"That dog is scared of cats," Fliss said. Fliss was Gunk's older sister.

"He's not scared," said Gunk. "It's just a lot to take in all at once, that's all!"

"Huh," said Fliss. "What are you going to call it, baby brother?"

"Spt," said the dog, looking up at Gunk.

"I'm going to call it Spot," said Gunk.

"Spot! What kind of a name is that?" asked Fliss.

"He looks like a Spot," said Gunk. "Don't you, Spot?"

"Spt," agreed the dog. He stretched his long neck up and slobbered on Gunk's chin.

"See?" said Gunk. "He knows his name already."

Fliss bent down to scratch Spot's tummy. Then she grinned. "I know something you don't know," she said.

"What?" asked Gunk.

"Your dog's a girl!" Fliss said, grinning.

CHAPTER 3

Spot Has Dinner

Gunk set the table while Fliss put frosting on Gunk's birthday cake. Spot lay under the table and peered out at Gunk.

They were having Gunk's favorites for dinner: salad, turkey with stuffing, baked potatoes, and chocolate cake. "Dinner's ready!" yelled Dad.

"What about Spot?" asked Gunk.

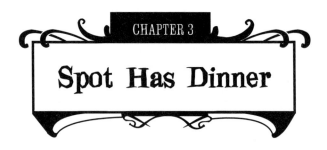

"There's dog food in the cupboard," said Dad.

Gunk opened a can. The smell of dog food filled the kitchen. Gunk tipped it out into Spot's dish.

"Here you go," said Gunk. "A delicious dinner." He crouched down by the doggy dish. "Come on, Spot," he said. "Dinner time."

Spot stuck her nose out from under the table. She wagged her tail, then walked slowly over to Gunk.

"See? Don't be scared. This is for you!" said Gunk.

Spot sniffed at the dog food.

Then she lifted up her nose and howled.

"No, really, it's nice doggy dinner!" said Gunk.

Mom wandered back into the kitchen. "What's going on?"

"I'm trying to get Spot to eat her dinner," explained Gunk. "Here, Spot!"

Spot lifted her head again. "Sspt!" she cried sadly.

"Why can't she howl like a normal dog?" asked Mom.

Spot took one sniff and two fat tears rolled down her big round nose.

"Come and have your dinner, Gunk," said Dad. "After all, it is your birthday dinner."

"But I can't let Spot starve!" cried Gunk.

"She'll eat when she's hungry," said Mom.

Gunk lifted Spot up in his arms and sat down at the table with Spot on his lap. Dad dished him a plate of food. Gunk reached for the salad.

"Spt?" said Spot suddenly. She poked her nose over the edge of the table. "Spt?" She stuck out her long thin tongue.

Gloop! A big leaf of lettuce disappeared into Spot's mouth. She chewed it slowly. Dad stared. "That dog just ate a lettuce leaf!" he said.

"Maybe she's a vegetarian," said Mom.

"There aren't any vegetarian dogs!" said Fliss.

"Spt," said Spot. Suddenly she climbed up onto the table and stuck her head in the salad bowl. "Spt, spt, spt," said Spot happily, gulping down a slice of cucumber.

"Well," said Dad, "at least we know what Spot likes for dinner!"

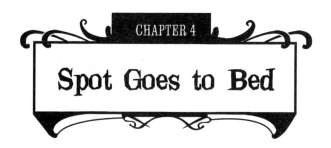

CHAPTER 4

Spot Goes to Bed

That night Gunk sat up in bed. Something had awoken him.

"Sppppppppttttttt!"

The noise came from the laundry room. Gunk pushed back his blankets and tiptoed down the hallway. He opened the laundry door and turned on the light.

Spot gazed up at him, blinking in the sudden light. Her big, bare nose was wet, and two more tears rolled down her chin.

"Spt," she said.

Gunk knelt down beside her. "What's wrong?" he asked. "Are you lonely?"

"Spt," agreed Spot.

"That's all right. I get lonely too sometimes," said Gunk. "Hey, do you want to come into bed with me?"

"Spt!" said Spot happily, slapping him on the ankle with her fat tail.

Gunk picked Spot up and tucked her into his pajama top to keep her warm. He tiptoed out of the laundry room and down the hallway toward his bedroom.

He placed Spot on the end of his bed, then slid under the covers himself.

"Good night, Spot," he said.

"Spt," said Spot. She snuggled with Gunk, her nose on his pillow and one paw on his arm.

Gunk closed his eyes. Five minutes later he opened them again.

Spot snored.

CHAPTER 5

Green Gloop

The next morning, Gunk stumbled out of bed and peered out into the hall. Dad was hopping around in his fluffy chicken slippers. He was trying to keep one of the chicken slippers off the carpet.

"What kind of dog leaves sloppy green doggy doo?" roared Dad.

"It's my fault," said Gunk. "I should have taken Spot out last night."

"Well, clean it up," Mom said. "I'm going to make some coffee."

She walked to the kitchen. A few seconds later, Gunk heard a scream. He raced to the kitchen.

Mom stared at the counter in horror. "She did it on the coffeepot!" she cried. "That dog doo-dooed on the coffeepot. Oh! It ate the rest of the lettuce too!"

"I guess that's why it's green doo-doo," said Gunk.

"I'll never use this coffeepot again," said Mom.

Suddenly there was another roar down the hall. The house shook as Fliss stomped down the hallway.

"I'll go find Spot," said Gunk, "and make sure she doesn't have to go again."

CHAPTER 6

Toilet Training Spot

Spot was in the living room. She grinned at Gunk with the stem of a rose in her mouth.

"Look," Gunk told Spot, "dogs don't eat roses or lettuce. They eat meat! Get it? And they don't do their doo-doo on people's teapots. You're supposed to go outside to do that!"

"Spt," said Spot.

"Yeah, I know," said Gunk.

He sighed. "You can't get outside. Dogs can't use door handles. It's my fault, but they're going to yell at you, too, so maybe we should get out of here for a while."

"Spt," agreed Spot.

Gunk threw on some clothes. Spot followed as Gunk ran out of the front door, down the steps, and around to the backyard.

"Okay," said Gunk. "Let's start toilet training."

"What are you doing?" asked a girl's voice.

Gunk jumped to his feet. It was Pete, from next door. "Oh, hi," Gunk said. He smiled. "What are you doing out so early?"

Pete shrugged. "I like early," she said. "There's no one around asking what you're doing."

"What are you doing?" asked Gunk.

"None of your business," said Pete. "Anyway, I asked first."

"I'm trying to train Spot. She's my new dog," said Gunk.

Pete stared. "That's the weirdest dog I've ever seen," she said.

"Spt," said Spot.

"She doesn't even bark!" cried Pete.

"I don't care!" Gunk yelled. "She's a great dog, even if she doesn't bark or look like a championship rottweiler. Anyway, who are you to talk? Who ever heard of a girl named Pete?"

Pete grinned. "No one," she said. "My name's really Petunia."

"It's what?" asked Gunk, then he blushed again. "I'm sorry," he said. "It's a nice name."

"Um, your dog is eating Mom's sweet peas," Pete said.

"No, Spot!" shouted Gunk. "I told you not to eat flowers."

"Spt?" Spot blinked, then hid under the bush.

She peered out nervously.

Gunk knelt down. "Look, Spot, I'm sorry I yelled at you. You can't eat Pete's mom's sweet peas."

"Spt?" asked Spot. She took a bite of grass.

Gunk sighed. "Okay, you can eat grass. Dogs do eat grass sometimes, don't they?" he asked Pete.

Pete looked at Spot. "Not that much grass," she said. "She's munching the lawn like a lawn mower."

"Well, we won't need to mow it then," said Gunk.

"You know," began Pete.

"Yeah, yeah," said Gunk. "I know. She's a weird dog."

"Actually, I was going to say she's a really smart dog," said Pete. "She looks dumb, but she understands just about everything you say. I bet she'll be easy to train."

"I hope so," said Gunk.

"Meow?" Pete's cat strolled through a row of bright flowers, then jumped on the fence and peered down at Spot.

"Spt!" cried Spot. She jumped into Gunk's arms and hid her face in his shirt.

"It's all right, Spot," he said. "The cat won't hurt you."

Pete looked at Spot. Then she looked at the cat. "I think Spot's very smart," she said. "Any other dog would just chase Mrs. Fluffytum."

"Mrs. Fluffytum!" said Gunk.

Pete blushed. "Mom named her," she said. "What do you expect from someone who named her daughter Petunia?" She glanced at her watch. "I'd better go," she said. "Good luck training Spot. See you around." She disappeared into her garden shed.

"Come on, Spot," Gunk said. "Let's go get some breakfast."

CHAPTER 7

Spot Figures it Out

Morning passed without any accidents on the carpet or the teapot or in Dad's slippers. Gunk took Spot out for a walk, carefully avoiding cats.

Pete was right, Gunk thought. Spot was smart. She trotted along on her leash and she didn't eat anything she wasn't supposed to. She also didn't leave any sloppy, green doggy doo behind her.

"Look, please try, Spot!" begged Gunk. "You have to learn to doo-doo outside."

"Spt?" said Spot.

"I wish dogs spoke human," said Gunk
with a sigh. "Or I wish humans spoke
dog. Come on, let's go home."

Gunk put Spot's leash away in the
cupboard, then headed down to the
bathroom he shared with Fliss to wash his
hands. As he was turning off the faucet,
he looked down.

"Spot!" he yelled. "What do you think
you're doing?"

"Spt?" asked Spot.
Her big, round
nose pushed the
toilet's handle.

She scrambled off the toilet. Shhwwwww! flushed the toilet.

So Gunk had a dog who did its doo-doo in the toilet and then flushed it afterward. So what? It was better than doing it in Mom's kitchen. Or on the lawn. In fact, it was really great that Spot had watched him and learned to be the neatest, tidiest dog in the universe. It was just that he wasn't sure everyone else would think so.

"Spt," said Spot.

"You're a good dog," said Gunk. "A really good dog. Just do it outside next time, all right? Now, this is how you wash your hands."

CHAPTER 8

Life with Spot

Life with Spot soon settled down. Every morning Gunk gave her a big bowl of lettuce to eat while he ate his cereal.

Every day Spot played in the garden and munched the grass till Gunk came home from school. Then, in the afternoon, they'd go for a walk together. For dinner Spot would have more lettuce.

It was good to get home to Spot's welcoming bark.

Not that she did bark, of course. She just said, "Spt," which Gunk thought meant, "Hey, am I glad to see you, Gunk!" in Spot language.

Spot was growing, too. Gunk hadn't realized anyone could grow so large just from eating lettuce. There was hardly room for both him and Spot in bed anymore.

"There's not room in this kitchen for us and that dog!" exclaimed Dad one morning. Spot was in the way as she munched her breakfast of lettuce and cucumber.

"Come on, Spot. Under the table!" ordered Gunk.

Spot sat down under the table to eat. She lifted her head as Mom wandered in.

"Hey!" yelled Fliss as her food slid off the table.

"Down, Spot!" cried Gunk.

Dad shook his head. "Spot will have to eat outside," he decided. "I never realized one small dog could grow so big!"

"Come on, Spot. You can finish your breakfast outside," said Gunk.

"Spt," said Spot. She trotted out after him and began to eat her lettuce again.

Pete peered at them through the sweet peas on her side of the fence. "I think she's a great dog," said Pete.

Gunk stared. "Spot? Everyone else says she's weird!"

"Well, she doesn't look quite like other dogs. There's something about her I really like. She sort of reminds me of something, but I can't think what. She's cute, anyway," decided Pete.

"See you later," said Pete. "I'd better get to work." She vanished into the shed.

Gunk bent down and patted Spot's hairy head. "See you, Spot," he said. "I have to go to football practice."

"Spt?" asked Spot.

Gunk shook his head. "I can't take you to football practice," he said. "There's too much shouting. You'd get scared."

"Spt," said Spot. Her eyes grew big and her tail drooped sadly as she watched Gunk walk down the street.

CHAPTER 9

Spot Can't Sleep

A year later, it was Gunk's birthday again. He got a computer game from Mom, pajamas with baby bunnies on them from Dad, a coupon for a free tattoo from Fliss, and a new bed.

"I don't know how you broke your old one!" said Mom.

No one knew Spot still slept on his bed — well, what was left of his bed. Spot was taller than Gunk, but still nervous about sleeping alone.

Spot had changed in other ways, too. Her neck had grown longer and her tail even fatter and her legs looked more like an elephant's than a dog's. Even worse, now that she was a year old, her fur was falling out.

"Your dog's going bald," said Fliss one morning. "You'll have to change her name to Egghead instead."

"Maybe she has fleas," said Dad.

"She's not scratching," said Gunk. "Some dogs are naturally bald."

"Yeah, but naturally bald dogs are the size of rats," said Fliss, "not baby elephants."

Mom shook her head. "Do you know how much it costs to feed that dog?" she asked.

"Look, I'm sorry!" yelled Gunk. "Spot can't help losing her hair, or eating so much food, or getting so big! It's not fair! Fliss has her motorcycle and Mom has her computer and Dad has his butterfly collection. All I have is Spot!"

"And enough dog hair to open a carpet factory and enough doggy drool to fill a bathtub," remarked Fliss. "Settle down, baby brother. No one's attacking your precious doggy. See you later, everyone." She clomped out.

The trouble came two days later. Gunk waited till everyone was asleep, then tiptoed to the laundry room. "Come on, Spot," he called. "Bedtime."

"Spt," said Spot.

She squeezed into the kitchen, bending her long neck so that her head could fit under the archway. She waddled in.

"Spt!" said Spot.

"What's wrong?" Gunk turned around. Spot gazed at him from the doorway.

"What is it?" asked Gunk. "You fit through the door yesterday! You can't have grown that much in one day!"

"Spt," said Spot sadly, drooling onto the carpet.

"You've been eating too much lettuce," cried Gunk. "Come on, breathe in!"

Spot breathed in. She tried to force herself through the doorway again.

"Stop!" cried Gunk. Spot was just too big. Gunk sighed and reached up to pet Spot's big, bald nose. "You'll just have to sleep in the laundry room," said Gunk. "You'll be all right," he added. "I'll only be a couple of rooms away."

"Spt," said Spot sadly. She turned around and walked back to the laundry room. Gunk followed her.

"Now go to sleep," he ordered. "Good night."

"Spt," sniffed Spot. Gunk turned to go back to his bedroom.

Gunk looked back at Spot. Big tears rolled down her nose and dripped onto the laundry floor. "Spot!" cried Gunk. "You're old enough to sleep by yourself."

"Spt," agreed Spot, laying her giant head on her blanket. She sniffed twice and stared sadly at Gunk.

"Good night, Spot," said Gunk.

He marched back to his room and climbed into bed. It seemed too big and empty without Spot. It was also too quiet without Spot snoring next to him. Gunk tossed and tried to get comfortable. Spot was all right! She was probably asleep by now. There was no point in worrying.

Gunk sighed, pushed back the blankets, and tiptoed out to the laundry room. There in the moonlight was Spot, sobbing quietly into the blanket.

"Oh, Spot!" said Gunk.

Gunk thought for a minute, then ran back to his bedroom. He grabbed his pillow and blanket, then crept back to the laundry room.

"Move over, you silly dog," he said, snuggling next to Spot. "And don't drool on my face, all right? It makes me dream that I'm drowning."

"Spt," said Spot happily.

"And wake me up before Dad gets up, too," warned Gunk. "I don't want anyone to know I'm sleeping with my dog in the laundry room."

"Spt," said Spot, settling down beside him, one giant paw across Gunk's shoulders.

Ten minutes later, both of them were snoring.

CHAPTER 10

Disaster!

Gunk slept with Spot in the laundry room for the next three weeks, and Spot kept growing. One night, Gunk took his bedding out to the laundry room. But there was no sign of Spot. Gunk went to the door and stuck his head out into the night air. "Hey, Spot!" he called softly.

"Spt," said Spot sadly. She was sitting by the back door. She'd grown again. Her head was higher than the doorway now.

"What's wrong, girl?" asked Gunk.

"Spt." Spot stood up and poked her long neck through the door.

Gunk scratched behind her ears. "Come on. Bedtime, Spot," he said.

"Spt," said Spot. She inched forward and Gunk saw what the problem was. "You don't fit!" he shouted. "Spot, you have to stop eating so much lettuce!"

"Spt," said Spot.

"Well, you'll just have to sleep outside. How about under my bedroom window?"

"Sppppttttt!" said Spot.

"Don't cry again!" cried Gunk. "Let me think. There has to be some way out of this." He thought. "I've got an idea. Follow me, but quietly, okay?"

"Spt," agreed Spot.

Gunk crept out of the house and climbed over the fence, trying not to squash any flowers. Spot followed him.

Gunk tiptoed over to Pete's window. "Hey, Pete!" he called. No answer. "Pete! It's me! Gunk!"

The window opened. Pete's head appeared. "What the heck is going on?" she demanded.

"I have to talk to you!" Gunk said. "It's important!"

Pete sighed. "All right. But it better be good." Her window shut with a bang.

CHAPTER 11

The Secret of Pete's Shed

Two minutes later Pete appeared around the side of the house. "Okay, what's so important?"

"It's Spot!" cried Gunk.

"Spot!" Pete looked alarmed. "What's wrong with her? Is she sick?"

"No. But she won't fit in the laundry room anymore."

"I'm not surprised," Pete said. "She's huge! You'd never think she was once a tiny puppy."

"She's still a puppy!" cried Gunk. "I mean almost a puppy. She's scared to sleep by herself."

"What's she scared about? If any burglar came by, Spot could sit on him. Or drown him in dribble."

"She gets lonely!" said Gunk. "Maybe it's because there aren't any other dogs like her. She used to sleep on my bed, and then when she couldn't fit down the hallway, I slept in the laundry room with her."

"You slept in the laundry room!" exclaimed Pete.

"Yes," said Gunk. "Now you probably think I'm a real dope."

"Actually," said Pete, "my opinion of you has just gone up six thousand percent. I think it's heroic to sleep in the laundry room with your dog."

"You do?" asked Gunk.

"Yep," said Pete. "But if you're okay in the laundry room, what's the problem now?"

"Spot won't fit in the laundry room anymore! So I wondered if we could sleep in your shed. Just for a night or two. Just till I can make a big doghouse for Spot."

"No," said Pete. She turned to go back inside.

"Please! For Spot's sake!" cried Gunk. "I don't care what's in the shed! I won't tell anyone! I promise."

Pete stopped. She stared at Gunk for a minute. "You really won't tell?" she asked.

"Promise. Cross my heart and hope to die," said Gunk.

Pete bit her lip. "I guess I can trust a kid who'll sleep in a laundry room just so his mutt doesn't get lonely," she said. "But if you say anything to anyone, I'll never speak to you again. Wait here. I'll go and get the key to the shed."

A minute later she came back and fit the key into the lock. The shed door creaked open.

"Hey, what's in here?" said Gunk. "It's not going to jump out at us, is it?"

"No," said Pete. She turned on the light.

Gunk stared. "It's incredible!" he whispered.

Pete let out a breath. "You like it?"

"It's wonderful! You really did this all by yourself?" asked Gunk.

"Yep," said Pete. "Remember, it's a secret."

"It's so cool!" said Gunk, gazing around the shed in amazement.

"It's a rhoetosaurus," said Pete. "They used to be around in the Jurassic age. You know, about one hundred and forty-four million years ago."

"Wow!" said Gunk, staring at the rhoetosaurus. "What's it made of?"

"The frame's made of wire," said Pete. "Then I stretched aluminum foil over it to look like skin."

"I think it's fantastic," said Gunk. "We'll be really careful with it. Spot might be big, but she's very gentle."

"Spt," agreed Spot. She looked at the rhoetosaurus model. She blinked. Then she walked up to it.

"Spt?" she asked it.

Gunk laughed. "It's not real, you silly dog!" he exclaimed. "It's just a model!"

"Spt," said Spot. She butted the dinosaur gently.

"She thinks it's alive," said Gunk. "I suppose because it looks so much like her." Gunk stopped. He stared at Spot.

Pete stared at Spot too. Then she looked at the rhoetosaurus, then back at Spot. "Oh my," she whispered. "Do you see what I see?"

"I think so," said Gunk. "Spot looks just like the rhoetosaurus!"

"Your dog's a dinosaur!" whispered Pete.

CHAPTER 12

A Dinosaur

Pete and Gunk stared at Spot. "How could I have missed it?" whispered Pete. "A dinosaur living right next door!"

"It's because you didn't expect it. No one could expect it," said Gunk. "I mean, it's impossible!"

"But it's true!" cried Pete.

Gunk shook his head. "No, it isn't," he said. "Spot just looks like a dinosaur."

Spot rubbed her face back and forth against the fake dinosaur's side.

"She thinks it's her mom," Gunk whispered. "Oh, Spot."

"Oh, Spot, I wish you could tell us how you got here!" Pete cried.

"Spt," said Spot.

"Talk English, I mean," said Pete.

"I don't think we'll ever know how Spot got here," said Pete. "Even if Spot could speak English, she probably doesn't know what happened to her when she was just an egg. I mean, you can't remember when you were a tiny baby, can you?"

"No," said Gunk.

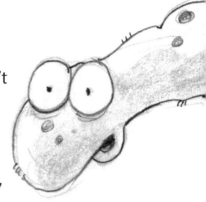

"Anyway, it doesn't matter how she got here," said Pete. "The question is, what do we do with her now?"

"What do you mean?" Gunk said. "You said Spot can sleep in the shed."

"No, how do we stop other people from finding out she's a dinosaur? Spot looked like a dog when she was small. But now that she's bigger and she's going bald, someone is sure to notice soon!"

"Why does it matter if people find out?" asked Gunk.

"Because if people find out you have a dinosaur living with you, they'll take Spot away to a zoo," said Pete. "Or lots of scientists will want to study her, and people will want to make movies of her."

"You mean I'd never see her?" cried
Gunk. "That's horrible! And Spot would
hate it too! She doesn't even like to sleep
by herself! She'd be really unhappy in
a dinosaur pen!" He stared at Pete in
despair. "What can we do?"

Pete grinned. "Good thing you've got
an incredibly smart neighbor," she said,
"because I've got an idea."

CHAPTER 13

Smart Pete

"What idea?" asked Gunk.

"Simple," said Pete. "We make everyone think Spot is a dog!"

"But they already think she's a dog!" Gunk pointed out.

"Yes, but we'll teach her to be even more like a dog!" said Pete. "That way no one will notice she's looking more and more like a dinosaur!"

"How?" demanded Gunk.

"Well, we can teach her to bark, for one thing, and make her a disguise." Pete's voice was bright with excitement. "Imagine," she said, "after all these years of studying dinosaurs, making model dinosaurs, dreaming about dinosaurs, I've actually got a real one in my shed!"

"Spt," said Spot. She yawned and snuggled down near the dinosaur model. Ten seconds later, she was asleep.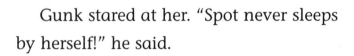

Gunk stared at her. "Spot never sleeps by herself!" he said.

"She's got another rhoetosaurus now for company," said Pete gently. "Get some sleep. I will too. We've got a big day tomorrow!"

Gunk woke up early the next morning. It had been hard falling asleep without Spot, but at least she was happy with her dinosaur friend. Had last night really happened?

Gunk threw his clothes on, dashed outside, jumped over the fence, and opened the shed door. Pete was already there with Spot.

"Hi," said Pete. "I had an idea!"

"Another one?" said Gunk.

"Yep. Someone's going to get suspicious if your mom keeps buying bag and bags of lettuce all the time. So why don't we take turns walking Spot after dark when no one's looking?"

"What good will that do?" asked Gunk. Somehow his dinosaur seemed to be turning into Pete's dinosaur too.

"Spot can eat stuff on the way. You know, the rose garden in the park and the flower beds outside Town Hall."

"But people will notice!" said Gunk.

"Nah," said Pete.

"What other good ideas do you have?" asked Gunk suspiciously.

"This!" Pete held up some fuzzy brown stuff. "It's fake hair, to make pretend beards and stuff. I thought we could stick the hair all over Spot, with extra on her neck to disguise how long it is. She'll look like a poodle, kind of."

"Great," said Gunk. "I'll have the only dinosaur-poodle in the world. A poodlesaurus!"

"And then," said Pete, "we have to teach Spot to bark!"

CHAPTER 14

Teaching Spot to Bark

Gunk had to admit that Spot looked different covered in hair. The ears made a difference too. Pete had made them out of cardboard and covered them with more fake hair.

Gunk put the finishing touches on Spot while Spot ate Pete's mom's straw hat.

"Looks great," said Pete. "Okay, let's get on with the barking lessons. It should be easy. Spot is so smart. We just have to show her how to bark. Okay, Spot."

"Spt?" said Spot.

"This is how you do it."

* * *

Four hours later Gunk was exhausted, Pete had almost lost her voice, and Spot still hadn't barked.

"You just go woof!" explained Pete for the fiftieth time. "It's easy, Spot!"

"Spt," said Spot.

"Give up," said Gunk. "Spot is never going to bark."

"There must be something we can do!" cried Pete. "Maybe we could tie a tape player around her neck with a recording of barking on it."

"Someone would notice," said Gunk. "Then they'd notice the fake hair. Then they'd notice that she is a dinosaur!"

"Well, you think of something!" demanded Pete.

"I have," said Gunk. "We'll only take Spot for walks when no one is around. I'll borrow Fliss's old tape player and we'll record some barks on it and keep it in your shed. Then when someone goes by, we can play the recording and they'll think there's a dog in there."

Pete frowned. "I suppose it'll work," she said. "Maybe we can also carry the tape with us when we walk her."

"Good idea," said Gunk. He frowned. "You know, I've been thinking. "

"What?" asked Pete.

"Well, you said your model wasn't a full-grown dinosaur."

"A full-grown dinosaur wouldn't fit in the shed," said Pete. Then her eyes widened. "Oh!" she said.

"Yeah," said Gunk. "What happens when Spot really grows up?"

CHAPTER 15

Woof!

Gunk worried all afternoon. "What are you thinking about?" asked Pete as they carried Fliss's tape recorder along the sidewalk.

"Oh, nothing," said Gunk. Maybe Spot wouldn't grow to full size for years. Gunk looked around. "How come there aren't any dogs out?" he complained.

"It's Saturday afternoon," said Pete. "Maybe they're all asleep. Hey, there's a dog!"

"That's Mrs. Finn's beagle," snorted Gunk. "It's too fat and sleepy to bark."

"Well, we can try," said Pete. "I've got an idea. You go meow! That'll wake the dog up and it'll start barking."

"Why can't you meow?" Gunk asked.

"Because I'm working the tape recorder. Go!"

Gunk looked around. At least no one was watching. "Meow," he muttered.

"Huh!" said Pete. "No dog would bark at that! Put some guts into it!"

"Meow," said Gunk.

"Oh, for heaven's sake," said Pete. "I'll be the cat. You take the tape recorder. Meow!" she shrieked.

Mrs. Finn's beagle lifted its head in horror and darted under the front steps. Mrs. Finn's window snapped open and Mrs. Finn looked out.

"What is it?" she cried. "Is someone being murdered? Help, police!"

"It was us, Mrs. Finn," called Gunk. "We're just . . ."

"Just rehearsing for the school play!" called Pete. "I'm really sorry, Mrs. Finn. I was pretending to be a cat."

"Cat?" snapped Mrs. Finn. "It sounded like a vampire attacking the garbage man!" She banged the window shut.

"So much for Mrs. Finn's beagle," said Gunk. "Let's try the dog in that house over there. I bet it'll start barking as soon as it sees us."

"Okay," said Pete.

They crossed the road and stared at the Great Dane.

"Come on, bark! Bark!" muttered Gunk.

"Woof! Woof!" said Pete. The dog jumped up and licked her face. "Gross," said Pete, wiping off the dog spit. "Come on, you dumb dog! Woof! Woof! Woof!"

The dog sat down and wagged its tail.

"It's no good," said Gunk. "It's just a friendly dog. I don't think it has a single woof in it."

"Well, I know where there's a dog that really will bark," said Pete.

"Why didn't you take us there in the first place then?" demanded Gunk.

"Well," said Pete, "there's just one problem."

CHAPTER 16

A Bark at Last

"Got the tape recorder on?" whispered Pete.

"Yes," said Gunk. "Why are you whispering?"

"Because," she said.

"Arf! Arf! Arf! Arf!Arf!Arf!Arf!Arf!Arf! Arf!Arf!Arf!Arf!Arf!"

Something small and hairy ran out from under the fence.

"Arf!Arf!Arf!Arf!Arf!Arf!Arf!Arf!Arf!"

"It's Nanky-poo. He's an Australian terrier," gasped Pete.

"Arf!Arf!Arf!Arf!"
The tiny terrier
sank his teeth into
Gunk's jeans.

"Let's get out of here!" Pete yelled.

They ran down the street, the small ball of mangy fur snapping at their ankles. It lost interest halfway down the road and turned back to attack a bicyclist heading the other way.

"Ow!" groaned Gunk. He bent down and inspected his jeans. "Look, the little runt tore a hole in them!"

"How about your leg?"

Gunk rolled up his jeans and inspected his leg. "No blood," he said.

"No big deal," said Pete. "We got our recording."

"No big deal?" said Gunk. "They're not your jeans. Okay, let's hear it."

Pete rewound the tape and pressed play.

"Arf!Arf!Arf!Arf!Arf!Arf!Arf!Arf!"

"Pete," said Gunk, "there's a problem."

"What?" asked Pete.

"That sounds like a rat pretending to be a rottweiler. We've got a dinosaur pretending to be a poodle! No one is going to believe that noise came out of an animal as big as Spot!"

"Maybe they'll think she's sick," said Pete. "You come up with a better idea!"

"I can't." Gunk looked at his watch. "I have to be home for dinner. Let's look for a dog with a real bark tomorrow."

"Okay," said Pete. "The recording is good enough to use tonight, anyway, when we take Spot for a walk. You still coming?"

"Sure," said Gunk.

Pete grinned. "It'll be so cool!" she exclaimed. "Imagine taking an actual dinosaur for a walk! It should be safe if we wait until it's really late. What could go wrong?"

CHAPTER 17

Plans

It was just growing dark when Gunk brought Spot's dinner out to the backyard.

"Here, Spot!"

"Spt?" Spot ran up. She had been leaning over the fence, so she could peer through the shed window at Pete's dinosaur model.

Gunk wondered if Mom and Dad and Pete's mom would mind if he and Pete took down part of the fence. That way Spot could get in and out.

Gunk looked at the fence more closely. The way it was leaning it looked like Spot would push it over soon anyway if they didn't take it down.

"Dinner, Spot," said Gunk.

"Spt," said Spot happily. She crunched a lettuce leaf in her wide jaws then gulped down another.

"I brought her some dessert!" Pete said, climbing over the fence.

"What is it?" asked Gunk.

"Chopped up sweet potato, six tomatoes, and half of Mrs. Feather's rose bush," said Pete.

"Won't she notice?"

"Nope," said Pete. "I said I was pruning it for her. She thinks I'm so sweet. Hey, I had a great idea!"

"What?" asked Gunk.

"Let's take Spot to the dump!"

"But we have to go through the center of town to get to the dump."

"We'll wait till really late, after everyone's gone to bed," said Pete. "It'll be dark then. Spot can have a real feast," added Pete. She hesitated. "Gunk?"

"Yeah?"

"Is it okay with you if I hug your dog? I mean your dinosaur," asked Pete.

"Okay by me," said Gunk.

Pete stretched up and hugged Spot's long, fat neck, then she stood on tiptoe and kissed Spot's big, bald nose.

"You're the nicest dinosaur in the world," Pete said to Spot.

"She's probably the only dinosaur in the world," Gunk pointed out.

"But if there were a million dinosaurs, Spot would still be the nicest one!"

"Spt," agreed Spot, drooling into Pete's hair.

CHAPTER 18

Taking Spot for a Walk

It was a long way to the dump. Gunk's legs ached, and the moon was high in the sky when they finally arrived.

"Ouch," said Pete. "My feet hurt."

"So do mine," said Gunk. "We'll get in good shape if we keep this up. Let's find a tree or something to lean against while Spot eats."

"Okay," said Pete. "Start chomping, Spot. You've got an hour to stuff your belly. Then we're going home to sleep."

This must be what the world looked like one hundred and forty-four million years ago, thought Gunk. Giant beasts like Spot feasting on the hillside, with strange trees around them.

What kinds of trees were there in the Jurassic period? he wondered sleepily. He'd have to ask Pete. But not now, later.

Gunk opened his eyes. He glanced at his watch. "Pete! Pete! Wake up!" he shouted. "We fell asleep! It's two o'clock in the morning!"

"Oh," said Pete. "That's all right. It doesn't matter if it's late. What difference does it make if we sleep here or at home in our beds?"

Gunk's aching back said it made a lot of difference. "Spot!" he yelled. "Here girl!"

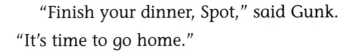

"Spt!" said Spot, bounding up to them. Her stomach was bulging.

"Finish your dinner, Spot," said Gunk. "It's time to go home."

The walk home seemed even longer than the walk to the dump. It was uphill, too. After ten minutes Gunk stopped. "I'm pooped," he said.

Pete looked back at him. "Well, unless you want to sleep on the side of the road tonight, we'd better keep going."

"No, wait! I've got an idea," said Gunk. "We'll ride on Spot."

"We'll what? You can't ride a dog!"

"But she's not a dog, she's a dinosaur!" Gunk pointed out.

"Well, you can't ride a dinosaur!" said Pete.

"How do you know?" asked Gunk.

"Because no one ever has!"

"Only because dinosaurs had all died out before humans came along," argued Gunk. "We won't know until we try."

"Okay, you try," said Pete. "I'll watch."

"All right," said Gunk. He gazed up at Spot. Maybe this wasn't such a good idea! He'd never even climbed on a horse before, much less a dinosaur!

"Spt?" said Spot.

Gunk breathed in deeply. What was he worried about? This wasn't just a dinosaur! This was Spot! Spot would never do anything to hurt him!

"Um, sit, Spot. Sit!" ordered Gunk.

"Have you ever taught Spot to sit?" asked Pete.

"No," admitted Gunk.

"Then you'd better show her how," said Pete.

"Look, you do it like this," said Gunk, sitting on the dirty concrete sidewalk.

Spot slowly sank down beside him.

"Good girl!" cried Gunk.

He scrambled to his feet, then carefully placed his legs on either side of Spot's huge body and sat down gently.

For a moment he thought he might be too heavy. Maybe a dinosaur's back wasn't as strong as a horse's back.

Slowly, Spot got to her feet. Gunk put his arms around her neck.

Spot took two steps forward, then bent down to Pete. "Spt?" she asked.

"I think she's asking if I want to climb on too," said Pete.

Spot sank down beside her.

Pete climbed onto Spot's back and held onto Gunk. Slowly, Spot got to her feet.

"Home, Spot!" said Gunk. Spot began to trot toward home.

CHAPTER 19

Danger

"This is incredible!" whispered Pete.

"Yeah," said Gunk. "Awesome!"

"Wow!" said Pete. "I'm the first person in the world to ride a dinosaur!"

"Second person," said Gunk.

"The first girl, then! This is the coolest thing in the universe!"

"Spt," agreed Spot.

They were back in town now. Not far now, thought Gunk.

Spot trotted around a corner. Suddenly she stopped. "Spt?" she asked.

"What's wrong?" Gunk asked.

Then he saw it. A car, parked right by the bank, with its trunk open. It must have broken down, he thought. He squinted in the lamplight to see who was in the car, and then he realized.

Bank! Car! Two thirty in the morning. The open trunk! The car hadn't broken down. It was bank robbers!

"Gunk!" said Pete.

She must have figured it out too, thought Gunk. "Let's get out of here!" he said softly.

"Spt?" said Spot.

Spot stepped up to the car and sniffed it curiously.

Gunk tried to tug her away. "No! That way, Spot! That way!" he begged.

"Hey, you kids, what do you think you're doing?" One of the men grabbed Gunk's arm.

Spot turned away from the car. "Ow!" shouted Gunk. He hit the ground. He looked up at the bank robbers.

Spot suddenly realized Gunk was no longer on her back. She turned back just as the robber grabbed Gunk and pushed him into the car. "Step on it!" he yelled, sliding into the backseat next to Gunk.

The car's doors slammed. The engine roared. The tires shrieked as the car sped away from the curb.

"They got Gunk!" screamed Pete.

Spot didn't hesitate. With one jump she dashed after the car, her giant legs pounding the road like she was a racehorse, with Pete clinging to her back.

CHAPTER 20

The Chase

In the car, Gunk gasped as hard hands grabbed his wrists and tied them together, then tied his ankles, too.

The car raced around a corner. Gunk turned his head. Behind them, Spot galloped down the road toward the car, with Pete clinging to the fur.

"Go, Spot, go!" Pete yelled. The wind grabbed her words and blew them toward Gunk. Spot's giant legs pounded even harder against the road.

Gunk gazed through the back window. Were Pete and Spot getting closer? Surely even Spot couldn't run that fast! The bank robber turned to look behind too. "Your little friend is trying to catch us." He laughed. "Good luck."

He was right! thought Gunk. Not even a dinosaur like Spot could catch a speeding car! If only another car would come to their rescue.

Vroom!

Gunk blinked. A car? No, it wasn't! A motorcycle was heading toward them with a person on its back.

"Help!" screamed Gunk, hope rising inside him. He tried to reach the window to scream again, but strong hands held him back.

The motorcycle passed the getaway car in a roar of exhaust fumes, then slowed down as it approached Spot and Pete. The rider pushed up the visor on the helmet.

It was Fliss!

The sound of Fliss's yell came faintly over the noise of the engine. "Pete? What are you doing?"

"It's Gunk!" screamed Pete, pointing toward the getaway car. "Bank robbers kidnapped him. He's in that car!"

"What? No stupid bank robbers are going to kidnap my baby brother!" Fliss yelled so loud that the words came clearly to Gunk in the car. "I'll go after them."

"No!" said Pete. "Go back to the bank! The police will be there! Tell the police where we are! Someone has to get the police, and Spot and I can't!"

Fliss's bike rumbled next to Spot. Then she yelled, "Okay!"

"Hurry, Fliss!" yelled Gunk. Fliss's bike made another U-turn and roared off back the way they'd come.

The bank robber pulled Gunk back into the car. "I told you to shut your face!" he snarled. He glanced back at Spot, then blinked. "What is that thing, anyway?"

"That's my dinosaur!" said Gunk.

The bank robber frowned. "Don't you joke with me kid," he ordered. He glanced back again and frowned. "Whatever it is, it's gaining on us! Better get a move on," he told the driver.

The car zoomed through the darkness, its headlights showing houses, gardens, then fields. Spot was a dark blob in the deeper darkness.

"Hurry, Spot! Hurry!" whispered Gunk.

Spot galloped into the night. There were no streetlights. Gunk wondered how Spot could see where to go. Maybe dinosaurs had better night vision than humans, he thought.

Gunk wiggled over to the window again, but the robber pulled him back. "One more peep out of you and you've had it," the robber warned. "Understand?"

Gunk nodded.

"I don't know what that thing is," muttered the robber, "but it's fast! Don't tell me it's a dinosaur again. I'll lose my temper." He paused. "You don't want me to lose my temper!" he added.

If only Fliss would hurry with the police! thought Gunk. He strained his ears for the sirens, but all he could hear was the thud of Spot's feet behind and the hard beating of his own heart as he waited helplessly for them to catch up.

Gunk could see Spot's face in the darkness. Her eyes were wide and determined as she strained after the car. He could see Pete now too, pale and frightened as she held on to Spot's neck.

What if Pete fell? thought Gunk. What if Spot tripped?

"It's nearly on us!" yelled the robber in the backseat.

Slowly, Spot came alongside the car. Gunk bit his lip. What could a dinosaur and a girl do against a carload of bank robbers? They'd be hurt for sure! Maybe even killed!

Suddenly Gunk didn't care what the robber did to him. He threw himself over to the window and leaned out again. "Go back, Spot! Go back!" he yelled. "It's not safe! They might hurt you!"

"Spt," bellowed Spot.

Gunk blinked. He had never heard Spot roar like that!

Whump!
Spot's giant tail slammed against the back window.

Whump

Whump!

In one swift move, Spot's head yanked the back door open. Her giant mouth opened, and she plucked Gunk from the backseat. Spot's big teeth gripped him by his shirt collar, and he swung back and forth above the road.

One final jump and Spot was in front of the car. Her tail swung again. Whump! The car swung as Spot's tail hit it. The tires screeched. Suddenly the car swerved off the road and down into the ditch on the other side. Its front stuck in the long dry grass, and its back tires spun crazily.

Then Gunk realized he'd been hearing police sirens for the last two minutes.

"Stop, Spot! Stop!" he yelled.

Spot stopped. Pete nearly flew over Spot's head, then recovered and slid off Spot's back, just as Spot put Gunk down gently on the road.

"Gunk!" shouted Pete. "Are you okay?"

Behind them, lights flashed in the darkness. Cars screeched to a stop, and they could hear the rumble of Fliss's motorcycle in the distance.

Gunk blinked. "Spot!" he gasped. "Are you all right?"

Spot was panting. She held up one foot and then another, as though they hurt. Pete untied the final knot around Gunk's ankles and staggered over to check Spot's tail. It was scratched and bleeding. Pete touched it and Spot moaned.

Gunk grabbed Spot's neck and hugged her hard. "Spot, you're a hero!" he cried.

"Heroine," said Pete. Tears were rolling down her face.

"Heroine," said Gunk. "Oh, Spot!"

CHAPTER 21

Discovery

Suddenly Gunk noticed there were cars all around them. Reporters! Gunk realized. They'd followed the police siren!

"What a monster!" cried someone. "Is it a dog? I've never seen a dog that big!"

"No dog ever looked like that!" said another voice. "Oh, my goodness." The voice was quiet with shock. "That's not a dog at all! It's a dinosaur!"

"It can't be," said the other voice. "Dinosaurs are extinct!"

"It is! I've seen dinosaurs just like it on TV! Look at that neck! That tail! Wait till we get this back to the TV station! We've got shots of a dinosaur!"

"No!" yelled Gunk. He tried to push Spot back. "You can't film Spot!"

The camera came closer, with the cameraman behind it and the reporter too. "Look, kid," she said, "this is the scoop of a lifetime! A dinosaur capturing bank robbers and rescuing a kidnapped kid! A dinosaur to the rescue! A Supersaurus! That's what we'll call it!"

"No!" cried Gunk again.

CHAPTER 22

The End

"You can't show that on TV!" said Gunk. "They'll take Spot away from me! Stop! Don't come any closer!"

The cameraman swung his camera toward Gunk, then back to Spot.

Spot lifted up her giant tail.

"Oh." The camera stopped swinging. The cameraman stepped back. The reporter stepped back too, just as Fliss's motorcycle roared up.

"Baby brother! Are you okay?"

The reporter turned to Fliss. "Hey, are you this kid's sister?" she asked. "Where did he get the dinosaur?"

"Dinosaur!" Fliss sounded stunned. She peered through the darkness at Spot. "What dinosaur? That's just Spot! She's my baby brother's dog." Fliss stopped and gazed at Spot. "She is, isn't she?" she whispered. "Spot's a dinosaur!"

"Now everyone knows!" wailed Gunk. "We tried so hard!"

Suddenly Pete began to laugh.

Gunk turned. "What's so funny?" he yelled. "If we'd never taken Spot for a walk, no one would have discovered her."

"Don't you see?" choked Pete, leaning against a fence post and trying to catch her breath.

"See what?" demanded Gunk.

"Fliss!" called Pete. "Try to take Spot away from Gunk!"

"Why?" demanded Fliss. She was watching the police put the bank robbers into a car.

"Please! Just try it!" Pete said.

"Well, okay," said Fliss. She reached down for Spot's leash.

"Spt," said Spot, quietly but firmly.

Fliss tugged on the leash. "Come on, Spot," she said. "Move." Spot stared at Fliss. She lifted up her tail. Fliss dropped the leash and gulped. Gunk had never seen Fliss scared before. But Fliss had never faced an angry dinosaur.

"See?" yelled Pete. "No one can take Spot away from you, or you away from Spot! She won't let them!"

A policeman coughed quietly, his notebook in his hand. "I'd say she's right, kid," he said. "I'd say that thing can do just about whatever it wants to. What is it, anyway?"

"A supersaurus," said the reporter.

"She's a rhoetosaurus," said Pete.

"My rhoetosaurus," added Gunk.

"You tell them, baby brother," said Fliss.

Suddenly something snapped in Gunk. The fear, the exhaustion, the terror all crowded together. "Don't call me baby brother!" he yelled.

"I'll call you whatever I want!" said Fliss.

"Spt," said Spot quietly, lifting up her giant tail.

Fliss shut her mouth. Then she grinned. "Don't worry, Gunk," she said. "People are going to want to study Spot and film her. But I don't think anyone is ever going to take your dinosaur away from you."

Gunk grabbed Spot's big round neck and pulled himself up. "Come on, Spot," he said. "Let's go home."

CHAPTER 23

One Year Later

"See, Spot? It's a book about you!" said Gunk.

"Spt?" asked Spot, peering down to look at the book on Gunk's lap.

Spot had grown in the past year. She was nearly fifty feet tall now. Her neck was longer than before, and her tail was even bigger. One blow of Spot's tail could knock over the school library. That was an accident and Gunk had promised the librarian it wouldn't happen again.

The title of the book was *Supersaurus.* There was a picture of Spot right on the front cover, taken on the night of the rescue, with Gunk and Pete looking scared behind her.

The book had been written by the reporter who'd followed them that night. Some of the money from the book was going to dinosaur research. The reporter had offered some of the money to Gunk, too, but he'd refused.

What with the film rights to Spot's life, the sale of Spot postcards, and the commercials for Dinosaur Dinners for Dogs, Gunk's family had more money now than they ever needed.

Gunk looked around the room. It was larger than the school gym. It had a fluffy carpet and the world's biggest sofa, big enough for a dinosaur to snuggle on and put its head on your lap.

Next to the sofa was a dinosaur-size doggy door. Outside stretched acres of grass and trees, and fields of lettuce and tomatoes and cucumbers and roses. It was just right for a dinosaur to graze on.

There was a lake, too, for Spot to swim in while the humans paddled their canoes and fished.

Suddenly Gunk's cell phone rang. He took it out of his pocket.

"Hello?" he said.

"Gunk, hi, it's me."

"Hi, Pete," said Gunk. "Hey, do you want to come over for dinner? Spot and I can come over and pick you up," he added. Spot bent down so she could hear the conversation too.

"Yeah, I'd like to," said Pete, her voice bright with excitement. "But that isn't why I called. Guess what?"

"What?" asked Gunk.

"I just logged onto the Supersaurus website," said Pete, "and this kid from China had just logged on too! He has a rhoetosaurus! They found an egg. It had protected the baby for one hundred and forty-four million years! I e-mailed him, and he's going to bring his dinosaur over here. His rhoetosaurus is just a baby, so it'll fit on a plane! And guess what?!"

"What?" said Gunk.

"His rhoetosaurus is a boy! So when his dinosaur gets bigger they can start a family."

Gunk grinned. "That," he said, "is the best idea you have ever had. It's the best idea in the universe! Hey, Spot! Guess what! You're going to have a boyfriend!"

"Spt," said Spot, as though to say, "I've got you, and Pete, too, but another dinosaur would be fun."

"See you later!" said Gunk into the phone. "Spot and I will gallop over in half an hour!"

"Great!" said Pete. "Hey, can I have one of the puppies? I mean dinosaurs?"

"Spt," said Spot.

"I guess that means yes," said Gunk. He said good-bye and stuffed the phone back into his pocket.

Gunk jogged across the living room and down the hallway.

Dad was in the kitchen, mixing Spot's afternoon snack. The experts at the museum had given the family a list of what they thought a rhoetosaurus should eat for a healthy dinosaur diet.

"One bale of hay," said Dad, "and then two dozen eggs."

"Spt!" said Spot, drooling onto the kitchen floor.

"Six buckets of seaweed, ten boxes of bananas, a watermelon. Down, Spot! There's a good dog, I mean dinosaur," said Dad.

"Hey, Dad," said Gunk. "Guess what? There's a kid in China who has a dinosaur just like Spot!"

"Oh, goodie!" said Dad. He looked nervous. "Another dinosaur!"

"It's a boy!" added Gunk. "Now Spot can have lots of baby dinosaurs! She can lay dinosaur eggs, and Pete and I will make sure they hatch, and we'll have dinosaurs all over the place! Won't that be cool? Dad? Dad?"

Spot peered down. "Spt?" she asked.

But Dad had fainted.

About the Author

Jackie French has written more than 100 books for children and adults, many of them award winners, including her 2003 ALA Notable Book *Diary of a Wombat*. French loves wombats. In fact, she's had 39 of them! She says that one of the reasons she writes so many books is to pay the carrot bill for the furry creatures. French is a terrible speller (she's dyslexic), but a terrific writer. She lives in Australia with her husband, children, and assorted marsupials.

About the Illustrator

Stephen Michael King grew up in Sydney, Australia. When he was nine, he was partially deaf, but no one noticed that he had a hearing problem. King turned to art to communicate without using words, and eventually his illustrations won him numerous awards. He lives on an island off the coast of Australia in a mud brick house.

Glossary

crept (KREPT)—moved slowly and quietly

despair (dis-PARE)—to feel sad, to lose hope

extinct (ek-STINKT)—no longer alive

graze (GRAYZ)—for an animal to eat grass or growing plants in a field or forest

heroic (hi-ROH-ik)—brave; acting like a hero

heroine (HARE-oh-in)—a female hero

inch (INTCH)—to move slowly, or just a little bit

mutt (MUTT)—a dog that belongs to no special breed, or else is a mix of several common breeds

rhoetosaurus (reet-oh-SORE-us)—a plant-eating dinosaur that scientists believe lived over 180 million years ago

suspicious (sus-PISH-us)—feeling or believing that something wrong or illegal is happening

ᥲ Discussion Questions ᥲ

1. How do you think Spot ended up in the animal shelter at the beginning of the story?

2. Why do you think Pete was nervous about showing people her special project in the shed? Was she worried about what they might think? Do you think she was afraid the model might get damaged? What do you think?

3. What do you think of Spot's disguise? Was it a good idea to cover her with fake hair? Why didn't people think Spot was a dinosaur until the very end of the story?

Writing Prompts

1. Would you want a dinosaur as a pet? Which one? Write a short story describing your dinosaur. Be sure to explain what it eats, where it sleeps, and what fun activities you do together.

2. At the end of the story, Gunk learns that a boy in China has a dinosaur just like Spot. Pete thinks the two pets should get together and have babies. What would happen next? Would there be lots of little dinosaurs running around? What kind of adventures would they have? Write a short story about Spot's babies.

3. What would it be like if there were dinosaurs on earth now? What would the advantages be, and what would the disadvantages be? Write a list explaining your thoughts.

⟅ Internet Sites ⟆

Do you want to know more about subjects related to this book? Or are you interested in learning about other topics? Then check out FactHound, a fun, easy way to find Internet sites.

Our investigative staff has already sniffed out great sites for you!

Here's how to use FactHound:

1. Visit *www.facthound.com*

2. Select your grade level.

3. To learn more about subjects related to this book, type in the book's ISBN number: **1598893440**.

4. Click the **Fetch It** button.

FactHound will fetch the best Internet sites for you!